MIDNIGHT PIRATE,

This Walker Double contains two very different, but equally entertaining stories for young readers – one about Hetty's trip to Scotland for a party, and the other about the kitten Ida befriends when staying with her aunts.

Diana Hendry is a poet and the author of numerous stories for young readers. These include the picture books *Dog Dottington* and *Christmas in Exeter Street*, the fiction titles *Fiona Finds Her Tongue* (shortlisted for the Smarties Book Prize), *Sam Sticks and Delilah*, *Wonderful Robert and Sweetie-Pie Nell*, *Flower Street Friends* and *Kid Kibble*, and the Walker Doubles *Hannah and Darjeeling* and *The Dream Camel and the Dazzling Cat*. She has also written two novels – *Double Vision* and *Harvey Angell*, winner of the 1991 Whitbread Children's Novel Award – as well as a volume of poetry for children, *Strange Goings-On*, and for adults, *Making Blue*. She tutors Creative Writing and Literature at Bristol University and in her spare time she likes to wear interesting hats and spin plates!

For George
(*Hetty's First Fling*)

First published
1984 as *Midnight Pirate* and
1985 as *Hetty's First Fling*
by Julia MacRae Books

This edition published 1996 by
Walker Books Ltd, 87 Vauxhall Walk
London SE11 5HJ

2 4 6 8 10 9 7 5 3 1

Text © 1984, 1985 Diana Hendry
Midnight Pirate: illustrations © 1984 Janet Duchesne
Hetty's First Fling: illustrations © 1985 Nicole Goodwin
Cover illustration © 1996 Allan Stone

This book has been typeset in Plantin Light.

Printed in Great Britain

British Library Cataloguing in Publication Data
A catalogue record for this book is available
from the British Library.

ISBN 0-7445-3683-9

Midnight Pirate, Midnight Party

DIANA HENDRY

Includes

Midnight Pirate
illustrated by Janet Duchesne

Hetty's First Fling
illustrated by Nicole Goodwin

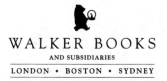

WALKER BOOKS
AND SUBSIDIARIES

LONDON • BOSTON • SYDNEY

CONTENTS

Midnight Pirate

1 About the Aunts 5

2 About Cleo's Terrible Nerves 10

3 About Some Very Fine Whiskers 16

4 About Nasty Pussums 22

5 About a Midnight Pirate 28

6 About a Different Pair of Whiskers 32

7 About Choosing a Home 38

Hetty's First Fling

1 The Invitation..43

2 The Journey 58

3 Little Chiefs and Wee Girlies 73

4 The Party 84

Midnight Pirate

1 About the Aunts

In November Ida was sent to stay with her two
aunts, Aunt Madge and Aunt Dolly.

Both Aunts were fat. Aunt Madge was fat in
the way of a wobbly jelly and Aunt Dolly was
fat in the way of a fresh baked bun. They were
both at least ninety and they had an old and
ugly bulldog called Cleo.

The Aunts' house was thin and narrow and
so cluttered with furniture and ornaments that
Ida held her breath whenever Aunt Dolly
steered her way, like a bus in traffic, round the
hazards of tables and lamps and vases to Her
Chair by the fire.

Aunt Dolly's chair was shaped to match her.
It had important mahogany arms, a round
wicker back and a broad, leather-buttoned seat.
Aunt Madge had a plain upright chair. Cleo

didn't have a chair. She had a sofa draped with patchwork blankets because, as Aunt Dolly often said, "We have to be very careful Cleo doesn't catch a chill."

"Now where are you going to sit?" Aunt Madge asked Ida on the first evening after tea.

"Perhaps a cushion ... or perhaps by Cleo...?" Almost all Aunt Madge's remarks began with "perhaps" and ended in the air.

"She can have the small rocker," said Aunt Dolly decidedly, and so the small rocker was brought from the kitchen and Ida, still in her best pinafore dress and white school socks, sat

between her two aunts and Cleo and felt very miserable indeed.

All three of them slept and snored.

Aunt Madge went "Hup! hup! hup!" every minute or so.

Aunt Dolly's snore was a long underwater gurgle.

And Cleo's was a snort.

Ida made a face at Cleo and sighed a loud please-wake-up sigh. But the Aunts hupped and snorkelled on. And as the evening wore on and the sky grew darker and the street quiet, the month of November – all the thirty days of it which Ida was to spend in Coppermill with the Aunts while her parents were in America – stretched and stretched like a quite small piece of chewing gum will do when you grip one end with your teeth and pull and pull the other as far as your arm will go.

Rocking gently in the kitchen rocker Ida remembered her mother saying, "Why, you'll have a lovely time darling! Aunt Dolly and Aunt Madge are perfect sweeties and their house is as cute as a doll's house." As she spoke, Ida's mother was sweeping up the sand which every day blew into the front hall from the seafront outside and managed to get everywhere as though it thought to turn the house into a beach.

Ida found she had a big ache of homesickness in her tummy. She tried to fold herself more quietly into the rocking chair. Five minutes passed, then ten. The snorers snored on. Cleo, dreaming of walks she used to walk, waved her paws in the air. Aunt Madge changed her "Hup! Hup! Hup!" to "Hip! Hip! Hip!" which came in squeaks from her nose. Very quietly Ida got up, crept out of the room and tiptoed up two flights of stairs to her small attic bedroom.

Her window looked out on a small garden in

the middle of the square where the Aunts had their house.

Ida pulled the curtains and jumped into bed quickly. The house was too warm and too quiet. Ida longed for the familiar sound of the sea, the boomy winter sound or the splashy summer sound.

Who wanted a garden? Who wanted a clean shiny hall without a grain of sand to tell you of other worlds? Who wanted quiet when sea noises could tell of adventures?

Thirty days hath September, April, June and November, Ida said to herself. Thirty long and awful days with two fat Aunts and a pampered old bulldog and no one of her own to love.

2 About Cleo's Terrible Nerves

In the morning Aunt Dolly gave Ida a large
bowl of lumpy porridge.

"Porridge is good for children," said Aunt
Dolly. "Makes them good and strong. Put salt
on it child."

"Well perhaps a little syrup might be..."
began Aunt Madge.

"Syrup on porridge is a sin," said Aunt
Dolly.

Both Aunts were wearing aprons. Aunt
Madge's striped apron seemed to have lost its
ribbons and was pinned to her person. She had
two big, clean dustbins before her and into
these she tipped:

4 litres elderflower blossom

3 kg sugar

0.5 kg raisins

3 lemons - rind and juice
and lots and lots and lots of cold tea.

And then Aunt Madge stirred, with a big wooden spoon, singing to herself as she did so, "O Susannah, won't you marry me?" The tip of her nose had turned red with her efforts and Ida, nibbling tiny quantities of the foul porridge, began to wonder if Aunt Madge were really a witch.

Aunt Dolly took a third tub and with a long plastic tube began filling bottles with clear, sparkling liquid.

"Whatever are you doing?" cried Ida, pushing away her porridge bowl.

"Making elderflower wine," said Aunt Dolly crisply.

"Making sunshine and rainbows," said Aunt Madge gaily.

Beneath the kitchen table Cleo lay on a soft, powder blue blanket with a pillow for her head. Ida knelt down and tried to tickle Cleo's tummy. Cleo snarled.

"Cleo has terrible nerves," said Aunt Dolly. "She's so sensitive."

"Perhaps I could take her for a walk this morning," suggested Ida for, although she could find it in her heart to *like* Cleo, she already felt as if she had been cooped up in this narrow, cluttered little house for two years, not two days.

"A walk! In this cold weather? Why even in her tartan coat Cleo would catch a chill," said Aunt Dolly.

"Perhaps round the garden," murmured Aunt Madge, "if the sun comes out...?"

But the sun didn't come out and Ida spent the whole morning in the hot little house with her Aunts. Aunt Madge kept adding a log to the fire and Aunt Dolly kept checking that there was not a draught from door or window that could blow on the delicate Cleo.

All morning they filled bottles with elder-flower wine and Ida was employed in carrying them down to the cellar where they glistened on the shelves. The cellar was cool and tidy. Jars of still-fermenting wine made a plopping noise like pebbles tossed in a pond. Large green apples rested on racks. A big jam pan hung from a hook. A net of elderflower hung from the ceiling to dry so that Ida thought the cellar looked like the flowery bower of a very practical fairy.

"Don't dawdle, Ida!" called Aunt Dolly, and
Ida had to run up the stairs for the next bottles.

In the afternoon both Aunts took a nap. Cleo,
with the deep sigh of one from whom life asks
just Too Much, staggered slowly from the
kitchen to the living room and, with an even
greater effort, heaved herself up onto the sofa.

"There, there, my darling," cooed Aunt Dolly, tucking Cleo in with an extra pink baby's blanket, "you have a nice sleepie byes." Cleo rested her head on her paws and raised her sad eyes to the ceiling.

Aunt Madge, collecting a number of cushions, melted into them. Aunt Dolly lowered herself carefully into her wicker and leather chair, folded her hands in her lap and waited for sleep to fall from heaven.

And then her eye lit on Ida, who, truth to tell, she had, for the moment, forgotten.

Ida had found a pack of cards and sat on the rug playing patience. Clearly she did not plan to sleep. It was very irritating. Aunt Dolly could see that Ida had found the Ace, King and Queen of Spades and the Ace and King of Diamonds, and the suspense of wondering whether the Jack of the former and the Queen of the latter would appear kept Aunt Dolly from sleep. And then whenever she closed her eyes she was disturbed by Ida's pigtails in their bright red ribbons wagging to and fro like two metronomes keeping time for a very jolly tune.

There was something busy and not at all sleepy about Ida's figure sitting on the rug. Her sturdy legs made you think of running and jumping, not of sleeping. Even Cleo seemed bothered, for she kept opening one gloomy eye to stare at Ida.

A distant memory came to Aunt Dolly's mind about children needing fresh air and she sat up briskly and said, "Put your hat and coat on child and go and play in the garden."

Ida, well aware that she was being "got rid of", put on her duffle coat and bobble hat, shut the door of the hot little house, crossed the street and went sulkily into the garden.

To a child who has had an endless beach for a playground, the garden in the square seemed a poor thing. It did not even boast a swing or a rubber tyre hanging from a tree. All it had was a bench that old ladies like Aunt Dolly and Aunt Madge might care to sit upon.

But it was in the garden that Ida first saw the kitten.

3 About Some Very Fine Whiskers

The kitten sat under a holly bush. It was the colour of black pepper and mustard except for four salt-white paws. Its fur glistened as brightly as the bottles in the Aunts' cellar and over one eye it had a black patch.

Ida knelt down before it. "Why you look just like a little pirate," she told the kitten, "you must be a sea cat!"

The kitten mewed and stood up, waving a fluffy tail that seemed several sizes too large for its body. It was so young that its legs wobbled when it walked. Ida laughed. "You haven't got your land legs yet," she said. The kitten sat down again and stared at Ida. Its eyes were as misty as a November sea, its nose like a knob of old soap. The kitten stuck this nose in the air and half closed its misty eyes as though it were thinking of great voyages across the ocean.

Ida reached out a hand and stroked the fur that shone like the holly leaves and flowered in a white ruff around the kitten's neck. Again the kitten moved away and this time Ida was

reminded of someone who has put on ice skates for the first time. The kitten wobbled a few paws and stopped.

"Haven't you got a home?" cried Ida.

"Where's your mother and your brothers and your sisters?" The kitten mewed, wobbled back and rubbed itself against Ida's legs. "You have very fine whiskers," Ida told it, "they must be at least three inches long and far too big for you at the moment." The kitten purred at this compliment to its whiskers. "Perhaps you'd like some milk," suggested Ida. The kitten blinked and twitched its ears. "If I knew where you lived I'd take you home," said Ida. "You're far too young to be straying in this way. I expect your mother is looking for you everywhere."

The kitten gave a small, experimental miaow.

Ida looked all about her, and the houses in the square, tall and silent, looked back at Ida. No face looked from a window searching for a small kitten – indeed Ida began to think that there was no one behind those silent windows but sleeping Aunts.

"I shall get you some milk myself," said Ida and she ran across the garden, through the gate, across the road to the Aunts' house. She

had left the door on the latch and now it was
easy to sneak in and creep down the hall to the
kitchen.

From the living room she could hear the
usual sounds.

"Hup! Hup! Hup!" – Aunt Madge.

"Snorkel! Snorkel! Snorkel!" – Aunt Dolly.

"Urgh! Urgh! Urgh!" – Cleo.

Ida took the milk from the fridge and set it
on the table. What to put it in was more difficult. On the Aunts' dresser was an army of
plates and cups and saucers but all of them of

the finest china, gold rimmed and flowery. Ida did not think Aunt Dolly would be at all happy to think of a kitten drinking milk out of one of her best saucers. And then she spotted just the thing. One of Cleo's bowls!

Now most dogs have two bowls, one for food and one for water, but Cleo being Cleo (and the Aunts being the Aunts) had five. A big one for her dinner, a big one for her water, a medium size one for scraps, a small one for treats and rewards, and a tiny pink spotted bowl for her daily vitamin pills. It was perfect! Just small enough and shallow enough for an unsteady kitten. And secretly Ida thought it was quite pretty enough too.

She poured the milk into it and keeping one

hand on top of the dish so that it wouldn't spill, she crept quietly out of the house, back across the road and into the garden where the kitten still waited.

Ida set the milk down on the grass. The kitten came carefully towards it, nose lowered, whiskers twitching. Then it crouched down and began to lap, its very pink little tongue rasping like sandpaper. Ida watched, her hands stuck in her pockets and a warm, happy feeling growing inside. As if the whole day felt the same way, a pale winter sun washed over the garden.

The kitten licked its long whiskers and looked up at Ida.

"I must go home now," Ida told it, "and you ought to go home too." The kitten stared at her seeming to wink its one
black-patch eye.

"I shall call you Pirate," said Ida.

The kitten winked again.

Ida walked away across the garden. "Go home, Pirate," she called to the kitten who still sat neatly under the holly tree. "If you have a home," she added miserably.

4 About Nasty Pussums

Ida found both Aunts in a terrible pother.

"Oh Ida dear, a most awful thing has happened," said Aunt Madge. Her hair had fallen out of its pins and strayed wildly everywhere.

Aunt Dolly, the tough and commanding Aunt Dolly, was weeping into a large mug of elderflower wine.

"Whatever is it?" cried Ida.

Aunt Dolly waved a large bottle of purple and blue striped vitamin pills at her. "Cleo's dear little pink spotted bowl," wailed Aunt Dolly. "Someone has stolen it and she'll never take her medicine without it," and Aunt Dolly dripped tears into her elderflower.

Cleo, meanwhile, sat beside her looking remarkably healthy and possibly pleased.

"Well I'm very sorry," said Ida, producing the pink and white bowl from behind her back, "but I borrowed it."

"Borrowed it!" cried both Aunts together, but not in the same tone, for Aunt Madge said "borrowed it" high up in the attic of her voice and Aunt Dolly said "borrowed it" deep down in the cellar of hers.

"Perhaps to play dollies' tea parties..." suggested Aunt Madge.

"Certainly not!" said Ida. "You see there was a kitten ... with such sweet long whiskers and a little white ruff and..."

"A kitten!" said both Aunts in the same attic and cellar voices as before and as much surprised as if Ida had said there was a dodo or a pterodactyl. "Yes," said Ida. "I found him in the garden, wobbling about on such shaky little legs

– he can't be more than a few weeks old."

"You shouldn't speak to stray kittens," said Aunt Dolly sternly.

"Well perhaps 'hello' is all right," said Aunt Madge hesitantly.

"No Madge, not even 'hello'," said Aunt Dolly. "Once you say 'hello' to a stray cat it's yours for ever. It's like a mother, someone who will love you even when you don't want to be loved."

"Well he seemed hungry," said Ida, tossing her plaits in a defiant way, "so I got Cleo's bowl and I gave him some milk."

"In Cleo's bowl!" cried Aunt Dolly. "Cleo's

very special medicine bowl that I bought at the antique shop?"

"It was just the right size!" said Ida. "How was I to know it was so special?"

"O poor Cleo!" soothed Aunt Dolly. "Did the nasty pussums have your very special bowl?"

Cleo let her head sag as though this was yet another blow of fate's which she had to suffer.

"He is *not* a nasty pussums at all!" cried Ida bursting into tears. "He is the sweetest little kitten I ever saw and much, much nicer than your fussy old Cleo!" And with this she slammed the kitchen door and ran upstairs to her attic bedroom.

Aunt Dolly and Aunt Madge and Cleo stood in the kitchen and shook in all their limbs.

Supper that evening was a very cold affair. Cold meat and cold feelings. Aunt Dolly clacked the salad spoons as though they were the snapping jaws of a crocodile. Even the salad cream fell in doleful dollops from the bottle. Just as they were finishing a lemon sorbet, so icy that it made Ida's teeth ache, there came a small sound at the kitchen window.

"Mew, mew," went the sound, then a scratch at the pane and "mew, mew," again. Aunt

Dolly, Aunt Madge and Ida, all with a silver teaspoon of iced sorbet halfway to their mouths, froze. Aunt Dolly put down her spoon, blew out her already large chest, strode to the window and without a word pulled down the blind.

"But it's Pirate!" cried Ida, jumping up. "It has to be Pirate and he doesn't have a home and he's hungry!"

"No, Ida," said Aunt Dolly sitting down again and chipping at her ice sorbet, "we are not going to have anything to do with a stray kitten. He's probably got fleas. And think of poor Cleo's nerves, not to mention mine and your dear Aunt Madge's."

"Perhaps a small saucer of milk..." suggested Aunt Madge. "He did sound like a particularly small kitten."

"No Madge," said Aunt Dolly, "Ida should never have spoken to him in the first place. We have no room here for a kitten."

It was a terrible evening. Aunt Dolly sat in her leather and wicker knitting a vest for Cleo; Aunt Madge sat in her upright embroidering a tea cosy. Ida sat on the rug between them doing a school project her teacher had set her while

she was away from school. *The Cat Family* wrote Ida and underlined it with her ruler. "In the cat family are lions, tigers, leopards and jaguars. There is also the wild cat and the domestic cat. The domestic cat came from Egypt." Ida put down her pen and began to draw a picture of the first Egyptian cat. Outside, in the cold English November night, Pirate the kitten mewed and mewed and mewed.

5 About a Midnight Pirate

Ida lay in bed and could not sleep. She heard
Aunt Dolly bolting the front door and Aunt
Madge bolting the back door and then both
Aunts coming upstairs. Aunt Dolly's bed
groaned twice, once for Aunt Dolly getting in
and once for Aunt Dolly turning over. Aunt
Madge's bed creaked and twanged for so long
that Ida wondered if Aunt Madge was unable
to sleep too.

She lay and listened to the distant sound of
traffic and wished it was the sound of the sea.
The house became silent. A church clock
chimed twelve. A cold, sleety rain fell against
the window pane. If Pirate was still outside he
would be very cold.

Without her slippers Ida crept quietly down-
stairs – avoiding all the steps that creaked – and

into the kitchen. Holding the blind by its small almond bobble she let it up very slowly. And there was Pirate, the sleet making his mustard and pepper coat look even glossier. He rubbed himself against the glass when Ida let up the blind and his small cries sounded tired and desperate.

The next part was even more difficult. It was a sash window that pushed up in noisy jerks. Ida edged it up until there was just a wide enough gap for her to reach out and lift Pirate in, holding him under his tummy.

She set him down on the floor. Pirate arched his back in fright and tried a few shaky steps on Aunt Madge's shiny tiles. Little paw marks began to appear every-  where. "O dear," said Ida, "whatever am I to do with you, Pirate?"

Pirate, spotting Cleo's five bowls ranged in a neat clean line, staggered across the kitchen to investigate and seemed to recognize the pink and white spotted bowl for he sat down before it and mewed.

"Well, I suppose I could wash it afterwards,"

said Ida to herself. She fetched some milk from the fridge and poured it carefully into the bowl. Pirate lapped and lapped until it was all finished. "You really are very hungry," said Ida picking him up and holding him close. Through her nightdress she could feel his little body throbbing against her.

"I can't let you starve," said Ida and she put the kitten down, opened the bread bin and cut a thin slice of bread. She broke it up into small pieces, poured on more milk and set it down before Pirate.

Again Pirate ate it all but this time, when he had finished he sat down and licked his paws

and whiskers in the satisfied way in which a man in a fine restaurant dabs his lips with his napkin. And then Pirate purred and purred and purred, and the next moment curled himself into a croissant and seemed ready to go fast asleep.

"Oh Pirate, dear little Pirate," whispered Ida, "you can't stay here. The Aunts don't want a kitten and Cleo wouldn't like a kitten," and shedding a few tears Ida edged open the window again and lifted Pirate out.

All the kitten's fur huffed with indignation and his tail wound about in spirals. He gave Ida one misty stare – as if to say "Really! you are very rude" – then he jumped down from the window sill and disappeared across the road and into the garden.

Ida let down the blind, washed Cleo's bowl very carefully and crept back to bed. Whatever would the Aunts say if they knew they had had a pirate as a midnight visitor?

But Pirate wasn't the only visitor that night.

6 About a Different Pair of Whiskers

The next morning when Aunt Madge went
down to the cellar for apples she heard a
rustling in the net of elderflower blossom. And
then she saw a tail whisk through the apples
and disappear into the darkness.

Aunt Madge gave a shriek, grabbed a handful
of apples and came up the stairs as fast as her
legs would let her. She twisted the key in the
cellar door and stood there panting.

"Whatever is the matter with you?" asked
Aunt Dolly, her hands and apron covered in
flour from the pastry she was making for
apple pie.

"Mice!" breathed Aunt Madge in a puffed-
out whisper. "Mice in our cellar!"

Aunt Dolly reached out for the apples and
found the proof. Each had been nicely nibbled.

"I've locked the door," said Aunt Madge shivering in her jelly flesh.

"Don't be so silly, Madge," snapped Aunt Dolly. "Do you think mice are going to come and go through the door? Perhaps you expect them to ring the front door bell?"

"All my elderflower blossom," sniffed Aunt Madge dabbing her eyes with her apron. "A whole summer's blossom. I think they've made a nest in it."

And while both Aunts stood staring at each other, a small brown creature – with whiskers of at least five inches – shot out of a hole by the cellar door, whizzed through Aunt Madge's legs, missed Aunt Dolly by a hair's breadth and fled behind the dresser.

Both Aunts shrieked. Aunt Madge climbed on the table. Aunt Dolly mounted the draining board by way of the kitchen stool and perched there, among the white breakfast cups and saucers, like an imposing stork standing on seashells. Cleo, moving faster than anyone had seen her move for years, dived into her basket and lay there trembling.

"I expect the mice have come in for the winter," said Ida helpfully.

"The winter?" cried Aunt Madge. "Oh dear me, I think they've come for ever!"

Aunt Dolly, still aloft the draining board and with her apron hauled up in case a mouse should try and follow her, found her most commanding voice.

"Where," she asked, "is the cat?"

There was a complete silence in the kitchen. Aunt Madge looked at Ida and Ida looked at Cleo and Cleo hid her head.

"W-W-W-What cat?" asked Aunt Madge timidly.

"Why *our* cat of course," said Aunt Dolly. "That little pepper and mustard creature who made such a nuisance of himself last night."

"What makes you think he's ours?" asked Aunt Madge.

"I've already told you," said Aunt Dolly climbing down from the stool, "cats are like mothers. You don't choose them, they choose you. Ida, go and find him."

With an enormous grin and with pigtails flying, Ida ran out of the house and into the garden. She looked under every bush and holly tree but there was no sign of Pirate. Ida called him by name and made odd pussy noises but still he did not come. Ida had to go sadly home and report to the Aunts that there was no sign of Pirate.

But secretly Pirate watched her from behind a dustbin.

Pirate was offended. He had not forgotten last night – invited in for supper and then, just when he was settling in, thrown out into the cold dark night. He would let Ida know that a cat was not a tame silly creature who would come when he was called, like a dog.

And so, only when he was good and ready did Pirate stroll – as well as he could on his wobbly legs – out from behind the dustbins, waving his overlarge tail as if he were in no hurry at all for lunch, and jumped up onto the kitchen window sill where Ida had been waiting for him all morning.

"He's here!" cried Ida. "Pirate's come!" And she pushed up the window and lifted him in. Pirate allowed himself to purr.

"About time too," said Aunt Dolly regarding the small kitten now planted on the floor. "In this house, Pirate, we have lunch at one o'clock precisely and perhaps you'll be kind enough to remember that in future."

For answer Pirate rubbed himself against Aunt Dolly's legs and purred again. From the basket under the table came a groaning moan. Cleo, still recovering from the mouse, could not remember a worse morning since the vet had given her an injection in her bottom.

"Be quiet, Cleo!" said Aunt Dolly. "This is Pirate, and you and Pirate are going to be very good friends."

7 About Choosing a Home

And so Pirate the kitten moved into the house in the square with the Aunts. He did not catch any mice but he frightened them all away and Aunt Madge decided to hang her net of elder-flower in the bedroom where she could keep an eye on it.

Cleo grew healthier and happier and didn't need any more vitamin pills. This was because she spent a lot of time chasing Pirate up and down the stairs and the exercise was good for her.

Aunt Madge had a holiday from polishing the hall floor because during these chases Cleo skidded, and having no brakes once went crashing into the front door.

Ida was happy because now she had someone of her own to love and to play with and Aunt

Dolly was happy because Pirate chose her bed to sleep on and, although Aunt Dolly did a great deal of "tut tutting" about this, she was really very pleased.

December came all too quickly. Ida, with her bag packed and her coat on, ready for the train, looked sadly out at the garden where she had first met Pirate. Aunt Madge and Aunt Dolly came down the stairs in their coats and hats. Aunt Madge had a big woolly bobble on her hat and Aunt Dolly three bright blue feathers on hers.

But Aunt Dolly was carrying a large wicker basket with a lid and a buckle at each side and the strange thing about this basket was that it went "mew, mew, mew".

"Here you are Ida," said Aunt Dolly. "It's been nearly as nice having Pirate to stay as it has been having you to stay, but I think Pirate belongs to you."

"Oh, Aunt Dolly!" cried Ida, knocking the

blue feathers askew as she gave her Aunt a
big kiss. "Pirate chose your house. He should
stay here."

"No, it was you Pirate chose," said Aunt
Dolly, "and you who fed him and you who
loved him. So being a very sensible cat he
decided that your home was his home."

"But you will bring him to see us, won't you,

Ida?" said Aunt Madge peeping in the basket for a last look at Pirate.

"Of course I will," said Ida.

So Pirate went home with Ida and there he became a proper sea cat for he walked on the beach every morning and ate shrimps for breakfast and slept in a sunny patch outside Ida's bedroom door.

And once a year Ida and Pirate went back to see the Aunts and Aunt Madge said they had never seen another mouse and Aunt Dolly said that Cleo had never needed another vitamin pill and they both said that Ida and Pirate were growing beautifully.

But Cleo only snored!

HETTY'S
FIRST FLING

1 The Invitation

The invitation to Great Uncle Fergus's party
arrived at the Mungoes' squeezed-in little
terrace on a Monday morning in spring.

"He's having a party," said Mr Mungoe in a
funeral voice.

"Whatever for?" asked Mrs Mungoe, snapping the toast out of the toaster as though the
two slices were the back and front of Great
Uncle Fergus, who ought to be toasted alive for
thinking of such a terrible thing as a party.

"Will it be on the island?" breathed Hetty, but nobody answered.

"I am not going," said James. James, aged fourteen, had not spoken for a year. Instead of words he twanged his guitar. C major meant "yes", G major meant "no". They got by. Now all the family looked at him. "I am not going," he repeated. "I shall never forgive Great Uncle Fergus," and he picked up his guitar from beside his chair, where it waited like a trusty dog, and twanged C major, G major, C major, G major, one after the other. (This meant "I am very upset.")

"Will it be on the island?" asked Hetty again.

"We'll have to go," said Mr Mungoe. "Uncle Fergus is seventy-five, he's asking the whole family. He says he wants to get everyone together before he dies."

"When's he dying?" asked Hetty. Hetty was nine.

"Twang!" went James's guitar in G major. (Never.)

Mrs Mungoe folded her hands in her lap and closed her eyes for a long time like one who has much to endure. "Off the beaten track," she moaned. "If Uncle Fergus were any more off the beaten track he'd fall into the sea. Mountain and moor and bog! Hay stacks where there should be shops! A hundred and one varieties of whisky and not a brown sliced loaf in sight." Mrs Mungoe was a town person. When she was out in the country she had the uncomfortable feeling of the world being unmade, as if God had not yet reached this part and had simply left the raw ingredients in a bowl to be cooked into streets and houses, churches and stations, when He had time.

"I'll buy you some climbing boots," said Mr Mungoe disappearing through the kitchen.

"Huh!" said Mrs Mungoe.

"Twang!" said James's guitar. (Ha! Ha!)

For a moment Mr Mungoe's face peered through the doorway. The gloom of his wife and son seemed to have cheered him up. He looked at Hetty sitting at the end of the table in her red dressing-gown with marmalade golly brooches marching down the lapel. "Yes," he said, "the party *will* be on the island," and he vanished.

Mrs Mungoe, who disliked mornings as much as she disliked the country, hid herself behind the newspaper so that just the top of her fierce red hair – Hetty's hair – showed, and waited for James and Hetty to go away, which they soon did; James to lie on his bed and twang dark chords and Hetty to her attic to look over the London clutter of roofs and chimneys and to think about the island.

Great Uncle Fergus's island was the Isle of Skye. Hetty had never been there and she had not so much a picture-in-her-mind about it as a feeling-in-her-bones. She thought it was as wild as Great Uncle Fergus's hair and as rough as his hairy oatmeal socks which he wore with his kilt, and as cold as his cheeks which, when she kissed him, felt chilled by mountain winds. Mainly what Hetty thought about when she looked out at the crowded London roofs with their curly red tiles or polished grey slates was all that space. The island, Hetty thought up there in her poky attic, was somewhere you could stretch and stretch and stretch, and never have to tuck your elbows in. It was somewhere you could stride with big long strides like Great Uncle Fergus took.

Hetty was the only Mungoe who liked Great Uncle Fergus and, in truth, Hetty didn't so much *like* Great Uncle as she liked to dream about his island. Great Uncle himself was rather alarming, Hetty thought, and so did all the Mungoes.

The trouble was that Great Uncle Fergus was determined to be a proper Uncle. He had no children of his own so he made up for it with other people's, like someone who has never been allowed puddings as a child and makes up for it by eating ice-cream ever after. Great Uncle Fergus made endless visits to those of his relations who had children. He didn't care for grown-ups or for anyone under six months old, but if you were between six months and four-teen years then you could be sure of a visit from Great Uncle Fergus.

It was a pity that Great Uncle Fergus had a dream idea about children (much as Hetty had a dream idea about islands) and that none of his nieces and nephews were anything like the child of that dream.

This child, a boy, liked museums, ice-cream, Battersea fun-fair, narrow-gauge railways and Westerns, more-or-less in that order and more-or-less all the things G.U.F. liked but which, on his remote island, he had little of. Worst of all was the fact that Great Uncle Fergus thought that every boy of the family would be proud to wear the tartan of the Mungoe clan. When James was ten, he had had made for him a kilt in green, blue and black tartan and had made James wear it all round town – to James's horror and the hoots of his friends. This was the deed for which James would never forgive Great Uncle Fergus.

At Christmas G.U.F. sent all the children boxes of pencils with their names printed in silver on each one, and on birthdays he sent Scottish pound notes which James changed as fast as he could at the Post Office, but which Hetty kept in a special pocket of her purse and didn't like to spend.

Once a year G.U.F. visited them on his way from the Mungoes in Chester to the Mungoes in Eastbourne so that Mrs Mungoe said that he must live very cheaply because there was always some Mungoe or other to provide him with food. But Mr Mungoe said this was unfair, think of the things G.U.F. bought for the children. At which James twanged a very ear-hurting chord which sounded like "kilts".

Great Uncle Fergus had been to see them last summer and stayed for a week. He had not mentioned a party then although he'd looked very old already. Hetty thought his scrawny neck seemed to be stretching for the sky like a giraffe's and his hair had caught the snow as the tops of mountains do. The Mungoes' small front room seemed to shrink as soon as G.U.F.'s shoulder, with its hump of knapsack, heaved through the door. Hetty felt as if a man from another world had arrived, bringing with him all that world's strange weathers. It was G.U.F.'s kilted knees that did it. Hetty sat on the pouffe in the corner and stared at them. It was easy to stare because G.U.F. never noticed Hetty. G.U.F. was only interested in the sons of the family (alas for James), his "Little Highland Chiefs" he called them.

Great Uncle Fergus's knees were pale, bare, bony and hairless. They looked very exposed, like two bald policemen without helmets or two babies without bonnets. Bare and daring were Great Uncle's knees and around them jigged the kilt with its savage silver pin, large enough for a giant baby's nappy, only this pin had a purple stone in it the colour of heather and was probably won in a battle with another Highland Chief.

Hetty imagined that there were still battles,
with swords, fought in Highland glens and such
big shoes as G.U.F. wore could only be for
leaping down rocky hills with a whoop and a
war cry.

"Well now," Great Uncle Fergus was saying
to James who, bribed by three L.P.s and a set of
new guitar strings, stood shiftily before him, "I

see you've grown out of your kilt."

James, who had never grown *into* his kilt
attempted a smile. "Hetty would love a kilt," he
said. "She's never had one."

"The wee girlie?" said Great Uncle, feeling
first James's calves and then what passed for
biceps in James's thin arms. "Ah well, her

mother can see to that. My job's to see to you Highland Chiefs." Great Uncle always called Hetty, "the wee girlie". Hetty wasn't even sure if he knew her name even though her pencils had Henrietta Mungoe printed on them very clearly in silver.

"Well, I'm not a very Highland person, Uncle…" James began.

"Nonsense, man!" said Great Uncle, squeezing James's frail and lowland arm. "It's in the blood. A wee bit of island porridge would soon stiffen that arm for you. Make you toss the caber!"

Neither Hetty nor James knew what a caber was and neither liked to ask; James because the answer might take half an hour and because he might be asked to toss whatever it was, and Hetty because she liked to imagine it was a Scottish chimney pot tossed in a vast frying pan like a pancake.

Great Uncle Fergus stayed for a week. He marched James round the British Museum, the Victoria and Albert Museum, the War Museum and even the Dolls' House Museum. He wouldn't hear a single twang out of the guitar and whenever James attempted the quietest "thrum" Great Uncle shouted, "Wheesht! Hold your noise, man! If you want noise I'll buy you bagpipes!" This threat kept James musically silent for the whole week.

Great Uncle Fergus insisted on soup every day even though the weather was hot. "We always have soup on the island," said G.U.F. "Cock-a-leekie, lentil, barley, pea," and Hetty went about the house singing quietly to herself, "Cock-a-leekie, lentil, barley, pea."

Once Mrs Mungoe said snappily that he wasn't on the island now and no one else liked soup, or not in summer, but G.U.F. threatened to cook a haggis, so after that she kept quiet although every night, when G.U.F. was snoring a loud Highland snore, she said to Mr Mungoe, "Little Highland Chiefs!" in a tone of great disgust.

Mr Mungoe almost always made the same

reply. "Well dear, he doesn't have a family of his own."

"He doesn't want one!" cried Mrs Mungoe. "He just wants a legion of Highland Chiefs. Why, he's hardly looked at our poor Hetty."

This was true. Great Uncle Fergus patted our poor Hetty's head about twice a day and said, "Here's the wee girlie." But that didn't make any difference to Hetty. She was the only one in the family who thought that Great Uncle Fergus of the brave, bare knees was a hero.

At the end of the week, G.U.F. got out the tape measure that he always kept in his pocket for measuring his Little Chiefs and measured James (armpit, waist, shoulder-to-waist, waist-to-knee), and wrote it all down in his little tartan book promising that James should have a brand new kilt.

After that he humped his knapsack on his back and, with his bare knees shining in the sun and his white hair bright as mountains in snow, he swung down the road to the station.

Mrs Mungoe and James danced a jig to celebrate and Mr Mungoe took off the tartan tie he'd worn all week, but Hetty stayed at the window watching the giant figure of Great

Uncle Fergus swinging down the road. The
garters round his socks had little tartan tags
that danced like butterflies about his knees as
he walked.

Only Hetty was sad when G.U.F. left and
only Hetty was glad when the invitation to
Great Uncle's party arrived.

"Will there be a cake with seventy-five

candles?" she asked her mother.

"There'll probably be cock-a-leekie, lentil, barley and pea soup," said Mrs Mungoe. "And haggis."

But Hetty went off to school thinking that they would toss the caber over the mountains and catch it in a frying pan on the other side, and that she would surely have a kilt with butterflies at her knees; she would run across the moor, through heather and through cotton grass and there would be so much space she'd be able to stretch and stretch and stretch until her fingers reached the very edges of the world.

2 The Journey

As it was, Hetty cried because she didn't have a kilt and James *nearly* cried because he did.

Mrs Mungoe said women and girls weren't expected to wear kilts but men and boys were, and it cost a lot of money to get to the island and a lot of money to hire a kilt for Mr Mungoe and Hetty had a nice blue party frock and that would have to do. Mrs Mungoe was so cross about the party that she said she was going to wear an orange dress which, put beneath her red hair, made you go, "ouch!" It was her protest she said.

James did a lot of protesting too. Mostly in A minor and D minor and worst of all, B flat minor. He sat in his bedroom with the blind pulled down playing the saddest chords he knew, until Mrs Mungoe cried into the frying pan and the frying pan fat sizzled and spat.

Just before the party, a large parcel came for James with a sea-blue post-mark on it saying "Isle of Skye". Nobody wanted to open it. It lay on the kitchen table for two days. Now and then Hetty rested her finger on the post-mark as if she might soak in the sea around the Isle.

Eventually Mr Mungoe persuaded James down into the kitchen and they opened the parcel. The kilt came attached to a white linen bodice. It was blue and green and black tartan and there was a big nappy pin with it, but the big pin didn't have a stone in it. Hetty thought that James was probably too little a chief to have a stone in his kilt pin and she wondered if all chiefs began, like James, by not wanting to be chiefs and what became of little girls who wanted to be chiefesses but couldn't! With the kilt was a hairy purse on a belt that Mr Mungoe said was a sporran, socks, and two garters with tartan butterfly tags. Hetty, her thumb in her mouth, looked at them with longing eyes.

James put on all his Little Chief clothes and stood before his family, his face a rhinoceros-sag of misery. "Cheer up, James," said Mr

Mungoe. "I'll let you dye your hair and put an earring in your ear when we come home!" James snarled an A minor snarl.

Hetty thought he looked wonderful. Except for his knees. James's knees were dimpled and round and friendly – not brave and bare. They were London sort of knees, squashed-up-on-the-tube sort of knees, comforted knees. Mr Mungoe's knees weren't quite right for his kilt either. They were very pale and unsure of themselves and the hairs stuck out in a startled sort of way as if surprised to find themselves without the covering of trousers. Mrs Mungoe laughed when she saw Mr Mungoe's knees in the kilt and said they were more like the knees of Highland cattle than Highland chiefs. She painted her nails as red as a double-decker London bus and said this was another protest.

But Mr Mungoe in his hired kilt, that was the same tartan as James's, had cheered up a good deal and began to swagger in a way that made the pleats of his kilt swing. And then he pretended his city umbrella was a shepherd's crook and strode about the kitchen making "Hoa! Hoa!" sheep-calling noises.

They were to travel to Scotland on the

overnight train.
It left London
at midnight,
and midnight,
on the day of
departure,
seemed to Hetty
as distant as the
moon. James
played the blues
on his guitar all
day. Mr Mungoe
taught Hetty a

Scottish dance called the Gay Gordons and
whirled her about the kitchen on his arm.

In the afternoon Mrs Mungoe showed them
the birthday present she had bought for Great
Uncle Fergus. It was an old map of the island.
They sat round the kitchen table and Mr
Mungoe read out the names of the places –
Talisker, Carbost, Soay, Vaternish, Dunvegan,
Ullinish, Portnalong, Portree, Torvaig. The
"ishy" names reminded Hetty of the wind or a
lullaby. Her eyelids drooped. "You can have a
sleep," said Mr Mungoe as Hetty's thumb went
in. "You'll be up very late for the midnight

train," and he carried Hetty upstairs.

When she woke up it was dusk. She looked out of the window at the low, smoky London sky. On the island the sky would be much higher than it was here. In fact that must be why it was called Skye – because there was more sky there than anywhere else – and there would be a space as big as Hyde Park in which to dance the Highland Fling and toss the chimney pot.

Hours and hours after the street lamps had come on and the first stars could be seen above the roofs, the taxi came for them. The West End flashed all its lights as they rattled past, Trafalgar Square tossed down its fountains like bouquets of raindrops, other taxis honked goodbye to them.

At the last minute, when they reached the station and got out of the taxi, they realized that James had somehow smuggled in his guitar wrapped up in his anorak. For a moment Mr Mungoe looked as if he might explode and his eyebrows stuck out like toothbrush bristles. But then Mrs Mungoe produced, from her pocket, her very special vegetable peeling knife (without which she was not at home anywhere), and

Hetty produced Panda (who should have been
in her suitcase but wasn't because he would
have suffocated there and, anyway, he wanted
to see what was going on). Mr Mungoe viewed
all these treasures and threw up his hands and
said, "What a family!" and marched them all
onto the platform.

The midnight sleeper was already waiting for
them, its helmeted head like a silver submarine

of the night. Mr Mungoe had reserved two
compartments. Hetty thought they were like
little cabins on a ship. James climbed up to the
top bunk and lay there, his thumb in his mouth
(although, of course, he was far too old for
this) and his guitar cuddled to his chest.

"Not a C major out of you tonight," Mr
Mungoe had said, so James just lay there, pat-
ting the guitar strings in a "there, there" kind of
way. But Hetty, wide awake, explored every
inch of the cabin.

Mrs Mungoe helped Hetty to wash and to
put on her pyjamas. "All aboard, sailor," she
said and Hetty climbed in. There was just room
for Panda.

There was a very small shelf on the wall
beside Hetty, and Hetty said it was a pity to
leave the shelf empty and Mrs Mungoe said
yes, if there was one thing she couldn't abide it

was an empty shelf. But it was too little for a book (which might fall down when the train was going) and it was just the right size for specs (if you wore specs, but Hetty didn't), so they settled for a handkerchief; and the shelf looked much better when it was full of hand-kerchief, and Hetty snuggled down to wait for the train to start.

Then Mrs Mungoe, with her red hair falling out of its pins, stood with her hands on her hips and looked up at James on the top bunk (with one thumb in his mouth and one arm round the dead body of his guitar) and Mrs Mungoe said, "When all this is over, James, I shall buy you six guitar lessons and another set of new strings." James did not want to look too happy too soon, so he took his thumb out slowly and climbed down the ladder and said maybe he'd put on his pyjamas now. And by the time Mr Mungoe came in to give them a goodnight kiss, they were both tucked up in their bunks and James had a packet of chewing gum on *his* shelf and the guitar slept on the lid of the washbasin with its mouth wide open.

Soon there was a banging of doors, shouts, a long whistle, a terrific jerk as if the sleeper had

indeed been asleep and woken up with a terrible start, and they were off, creaking and
unsteady at first and then gathering speed and
a regular rhythm as though a music teacher
with a baton were out in front saying, "Now,
one two three four, *one* two three four – keep
time!" And the train did and Hetty and James –

who at first thought they would never sleep with such a noise – soon did.

When Hetty woke up, the train seemed to be riding very lightly along the tracks and James was up at the window, still in his pyjamas. The blind was up and as Hetty looked out she saw first brown, craggy rocks going up, up, up and then, to her astonishment, a deer, its antlers – large and knobbly as the coat hooks in James's school cloakroom – set very wide and surprised and shaping a huge grin on the face of the hills. There were more of them as Hetty joined James at the window and each one stood and stared at the sleeper train with that strange, quiet stare of animals who own the land.

At Inverness they left the sleeper, and caught a small two-coach train to Kyle. And then came the ferry.

Chubby as a baby's bath boat, it had a bright red funnel, a shining brass rail and its name was *The Bonnie Prince Charlie*. Mr Mungoe told Hetty that he was the most famous Highland Chief of all and that he'd loved a girl from the island called Flora MacDonald.

Seagulls clung about the funnel of the ferry like fans about a pop star until a policeman of a wind blew them, crying, away. James and Hetty put on their cagoules and scarves and found a whitewashed bench on deck. They all huddled together. The funnel made a noise like a polite

gentleman coughing and then a rather ruder gentleman belching and then, as if it could not wait a moment longer, it gave a great hoot at

the sky and they were at sea.

After about ten minutes on the choppy waters James and Mrs Mungoe began to feel a bit odd. Mrs Mungoe turned so pale that her freckles stood out like stars on a dark night and James went the colour of old parsnips. They said they would go below so that they wouldn't

feel the boat rocking so much. Hetty and Mr
Mungoe snuggled together and Hetty watched
a man at the prow who was wearing a kilt and
whose butterfly tags fluttered very fast in the
wind. Mr Mungoe sang "Over the Sea to Skye"
in a low, deep voice and Hetty said, "I wish I
could be a Little Highland Chief and have
butterflies at my knees," and Mr Mungoe gave
her an extra hug.

Then all too quickly they were there and the
sailors were tossing out the ropes to other
sailors who were waiting for them and who
wound them round big iron cotton reels. There
on the dock with his kilt and his white hair was
Great Uncle Fergus, not looking quite so much
a giant out here where there really was a lot of
space, as he looked in London, but still, with
his straight back and his hairy jacket and his
hairy socks (and the brave warrior knees), looking very much a Chief. Because it was his
birthday he was wearing a sprig of heather in
his buttonhole.

Hetty, suddenly not caring whether G.U.F.
only saw her as "that wee girlie", took out her
blue spotted handkerchief and waved it like
mad. And G.U.F. grinned and took out his,

(striped) and waved it back. Then they all lurched and staggered down the gangplank, calling, "Happy Birthday! Happy Birthday!" (Mrs Mungoe and James rather quietly because their tummies were not yet back in their proper places.)

"Well, how's my Little Highland Chief?" asked G.U.F. ignoring everyone else and clapping James on the shoulder so that James's tummy fell two inches at once. Without waiting for a reply he turned to the others. "Well then clan, ready for the ceilidh?"

"What's a ceilidh?" whispered Hetty to her father.

"A party," Mr Mungoe whispered back and Hetty's heart went soaring like a seagull into the high, high island sky.

3 Little Chiefs and Wee Girlies

Great Uncle Fergus lived in one of the places
with a wind-whispering name. Talisker. He
drove them down the narrow island road and
Hetty saw the moors full of blue scabias and
cotton grass and here and there a small croft
crouched low under the big sky, each with a tin
shack painted scarlet or yellow at its side. Many
of the crofts had a large yellow bun of hay held
against the wind by a fishing net. Some of the
houses were thatched and the thatch was tied
down with ropes and the ropes weighted with
stones. There was enough sky and wind here
for a roof to blow "whoops" and away.

Sometimes they passed trenches dug in the
bog by the islanders for the peat which they
used for their fires and which smelt like brew-
ing tea. The slices of dark brown soggy peat

were laid along the trenches to dry and looked like enormous slabs of treacle toffee. Hetty looked everywhere to see if she could see someone tossing a chimney pot but she couldn't. The road was so narrow that when another car came the other way G.U.F. had to pull into a lay-by and wait for it to pass. But of course what was nicest of all about the island was that the sea was so close all around you. It held you in a hug and you always knew where you were because you stood within its arms.

G.U.F. turned off down a bumpy road that made Mrs Mungoe groan and say that *this* must be what was meant by "going off the beaten track". And by the time they'd bumped to the bottom of the track to G.U.F.'s tall stone house, all the pins had fallen out of her hair and Mr Mungoe said she looked like a red-haired scarecrow.

To the surprise of James and Hetty, G.U.F.'s house was a hundred yards from the beach of Talisker Bay. In all his talk about the island G.U.F. had never mentioned this. Probably the beach at the bottom of his garden was as com-monplace to him as the bus stop at the bottom of James's and Hetty's.

James and Hetty were all for ignoring the house – big and grand though it seemed – and running straight to the beach, but G.U.F. held them back. "Unpack first," he said, "then all my Little Highland Chiefs can spend the afternoon on the beach while we grown-ups get ready for the ceilidh."

"*And* the wee girlies!" piped Hetty. G.U.F. gave her an odd look and said, "Yes, and the wee girlies."

So they went into the house which had big grey flags on the floor and pictures of Highland Chiefs everywhere and a big goat's head over the stairs, only Mr Mungoe said it wasn't a goat it was an ibex. Hetty found she was in a bedroom with five other girls and that these "wee girlies" were all her cousins. (James, as one of seven Little Highland Chiefs, had a room to himself – the house was that big.)

All the "wee girlies" were ranged on the sides of their beds looking gloomy. "Well," said the largest of them who was fuzzing her hair out with a spiky brush, "*we* don't matter, do we? It's the precious Little Highland Chiefs who matter."

"I *won't* sing Happy Birthday, I won't!" said a

second wee girlie.

"I'll put a spider in his sporran!" said a third scraggy cousin with a brace on her teeth.

"I'll shove oat cakes down his socks!" said a fourth.

"I'll blow out all his candles!" said the fifth.

"And I won't toss the chimney pot!" cried Hetty, not wanting to be left out. There was a silence after this and Hetty was sorry she had spoken because although G.U.F. didn't seem to care for Hetty, Hetty cared for G.U.F.

Things were little better among the seven Little Highland Chiefs. Only one of them, Robin, lived on the island, the rest didn't even live in Scotland and none of them wanted to wear a kilt or be a Highland Chief. They wanted jeans and discos and guitars and motorbikes. They ganged together on the beach that afternoon, sitting round an old crate set on the black sand, and looking like a plot of pirates hunched over the treasure map of their miseries.

Indeed it was a very pirate-like beach, surrounded by cliffs and with a wind so strong that the thirty-foot waterfall blew upwards, as if they were in a strange magic land where water-

falls blew upwards and white sand became
black. The beach was littered with the bones of
lost sheep, boxes with foreign names burnt on

their sides, crates and orange and blue ropes
from ships which Hetty felt sure had been
wrecked there. Above the cliffs hooded crows
waged war on four buzzards.

Only Robin wandered off to watch the battle,
climbing easily over the rocks with his binocu-
lars hung round his neck. He moved with the
freedom of a boy who has always known a lot
of space. Hetty thought he made all the other
boys look cramped in their clothes. Robin wore
his kilt as easily as James wore jeans.

Once Robin clambered down to where Hetty
was writing on the sand with the tip of a gull's

feather. He stood over her, watching – a tall, serious boy with a face that expected surprises.

"Yesterday I saw the death cart," he said abruptly.

HAPPY BIRTH, wrote Hetty in the sand.

"It's all black," said Robin, "and when you

see it, it means someone's going to die."

"Great Uncle Fergus?" asked Hetty, alarmed. Robin shrugged. "Who knows?" he said mysteriously. "It might be me, it might be you, it might be anyone."

DAY GREAT UNCLE, Hetty continued determinedly, as though writing it might make sure it *wasn't* Great Uncle Fergus who got carried away in the death cart.

"Do you believe in fairies?" Robin asked, just as abruptly. Hetty hesitated. James, she knew, would sneer at fairies and so would all her friends. But Robin was somehow different. His mind wasn't tied down with ropes and stones like the thatched roofs. Wind and sky had blown into it. Wind and sky, dreams and fairies, buzzards and crows and death carts.

"Well, yes I do," said Hetty. "Do you?"

"Oh yes," said Robin easily. "I've seen them."

FERGUS, wrote Hetty with triumph. But before she had time to ask any more questions Great Uncle Fergus himself appeared, standing on a rock near the house and banging a loud brass gong. It was time to go in.

Somehow the gong was like raw excitement sent straight to their party spirits. But the Little

Chiefs were not to be won so easily. They
slouched into the house, their hands in their
pockets. The girls who, for a brief hour, had
become Joanne, Charlotte, Alice, Julia and
Marie, remembered that they were nameless
wee girlies again and lost their smiles.

If it hadn't been for the swing of Robin's kilt
and the brightness of Hetty's eyes, you would
never have guessed that Great Uncle Fergus's
amazing Highland party was about to begin.

4 The Party

It was said that on the night of Great Uncle
Fergus's party the lights from his house could
be seen in Portree and the noise of bagpipes
and fiddles could be heard on the mainland.

Everyone came. The whole clan. There was
G.U.F.'s important brother, The Hon.
Alexander Ian Lachlan Mungoe M.P. – known
as The Eagle of the North. There were three
nephews who came all the way from their
sheep farm in Australia in their woolly jerseys.
There were forty-five cousins who were once
removed and twice removed and thrice
removed and more times removed than anyone
could ever work out. There was Aunt
Euphemia who had not been beyond her front
door since 1965 and who came in a purple
Rolls Royce with a hot water-bottle tied round

her middle. There was Murdo Mungoe the sailor, and Mungo Mungoe the vet, and Aunt Morag Agnes Mungoe whose dangling earrings nearly touched the floor.

When the gang of Little Chiefs came down in their kilts (looking like prisoners of war), and the wee girlies came down (pretty on the outside and snarling on the in), they found the doors of the main rooms flung open and they all opened their mouths wide and said, "Oooooooh!"

Great Uncle Fergus had hired disco lights. The room moved with all the colours of a paintbox. It was like walking on a planet where multi-coloured moons swam around you. In one room a table as long as the clan itself was draped with Scottish flags and set in the centre was a great silver tureen of raspberry ice-cream chilled by small icebergs. On the right was the cake, all seventy-five layers of it, like a sandwich for a giant, with chocolate butter icing oozing out of the sides of it and seventy-five candles crowded on the top of it. On the left was an enormous purple jelly, the colour of Aunt Euphemia's Rolls Royce, moulded into the shape of the Loch Ness Monster.

In the moon room, as Hetty called it to herself, the bagpipers and fiddlers took it in turn
to play the Strathspey Reel and the Duke of
Perth and, between two crossed swords, the
Hon. Alexander danced a neat and nimble
sword dance.

No one, until that night, had guessed that
Great Uncle Fergus was so good at giving
parties. He was good at giving them because
his life on the island, with its long, dark winters,
was such a quiet one that, when he *did* have a
party, he wanted it to be the loudest, brightest,
biggest, *Chiefest* party ever known. And it was.

Everyone danced and drank and ate Loch
Ness Monster Jelly and Iceberg Ice-cream and
greeted their long lost cousins – four-times-
removed and Hetty danced a Foursome Reel

with Murdo and Mungo and Morag and the Dashing White Sergeant with Robin. Robin cupped his hands round her ear and above the noise of the bagpipes shouted, "There's still a surprise to come!"

But despite all this fun, everyone was still a bit afraid of Great Uncle Fergus. Maybe it was because he was bigger than anyone else and his clothes were prickly and so was his temper. Whatever it was, when G.U.F. banged his golden gong as though he rang the northern star and said, "Ladies and Gentlemen, it is time for the Gay Gordons – which of you fine ladies will be my partner?" there was a sudden silence. The fiddlers held their bows against their fiddles, the bagpipers rested their elbows on their bags. Mr Mungoe pinched Mrs Mungoe but she pretended not to notice.

Then Hetty could bear it no longer. She marched across the multi-coloured moon room in her Skye-blue party dress and said, "I'll be your partner, Great Uncle Fergus." And Great Uncle Fergus said, "Who are you?" because he couldn't tell one wee girlie from another, they were all just names on pencils to him. Hetty said very firmly, "I am Hetty," and G.U.F. said,

"Hetty! Oh yes, you waved your spotty hankie
to me." Then everyone laughed and clapped
and made up a set for the Gay Gordons and in
between swopping partners and whirling round
and round, Hetty managed to tell Great Uncle
Fergus how much she'd wanted a kilt (and particularly the butterfly bits round the socks), and
how she'd wanted to dance the Gay Gordons

out in the open so that she could stretch and stretch and stretch and not have to tuck her elbows in. And G.U.F. told her she was a funny wee girlie and Hetty reminded him that her name was Hetty.

By then it was nearly midnight and G.U.F. banged the gong again and told them that there was one last surprise (Robin winked at Hetty) and they were all to go down to the beach. When they got there they saw a huge bonfire, tall as the waterfall, blazing up to the high Skye sky.

The fiddlers came down to the beach too, struggling with their music against roar of water and crackle of flame. Before they began to play, Great Uncle Fergus climbed onto a rock and said, "Now, clan, we are going to dance the Gay Gordons one more time – and this time especially for Hetty!" Then he got off his rock, walked over to Hetty, bowed and said, "May I have the pleasure?" And Hetty said, "Delighted," which she thought was the proper thing to say. Then the Little Chiefs – who had been having such a good time they'd forgotten they were wearing kilts – and the wee girlies – now pretty inside and out – stripped off their

shoes and socks and all the grown-ups followed
their example, and they all danced the Gay
Gordons on the beach in flame light and wave
light to the faint, fairy-like sound of the fiddles.

Hetty swung from partner to partner with all
the space in the world to dance in. Once she
whirled round with her arm crooked in Robin's
who went so fast that Hetty got dizzy and

thought her feet might leave the sand and fly
her to the top of the waterfall.

When that was over they all joined hands
round the bonfire and sang "Happy Birthday"
at the tops of their voices. While they were
doing this, Aunt Morag and Aunt Euphemia
turned the lights of the house off and lit the
candles on the cake so that when they went
inside they were all hushed by the sudden,

silent delight of so many candles. But Great Uncle Fergus cried, "This is a party!" and switched the disco lights on again and cut the seventy-five-layered cake into hundreds of slices (Uncle Murdo had five and Mungo had sixteen), so that by the time they all fell into bed at the end of the party, there wasn't a lick of chocolate butter icing left.

The next morning, while everyone else was still asleep, Hetty looked out of her window and saw Robin herding the cows to the top of the hill. She crept out of bed and down the stairs. The house looked as topsy-turvy as if a horde of elfin shoemakers had been working there all night. Outside, in the brisk morning air, the world looked suddenly sensible and everyday-ish, as if there had never been a party with Loch Ness Monster jelly and a room full of coloured moons. Hetty went to sit on a gate which turned out to be an old brass bed-head. Perhaps the world wasn't so every-dayish after all.

Soon the vet and his assistant arrived in a Land Rover and Robin came to sit beside Hetty on the bed-head gate.

"He's come to give the cows an injection,"

said Robin. "It keeps their milk pure."

Hetty studied Robin's bare, brave knees.

"Could you show me the fairies?" she said at last.

"I couldn't do that," said Robin. "Fairies are something you see for yourself or you don't see at all."

Hetty said nothing but two tears plopped onto her own bare, brave knees.

"Oh," said Robin, "you mustn't cry about it. I expect you will see them one day. You're the type."

"Really?" said Hetty.

"Oh aye," said Robin comfortably. "Tell you what though, I'll give you my butterfly tags. Great Uncle told me you'd taken a fancy to them." And Robin lifted the tops of his socks and pulled off his garters and gave them to Hetty. They were too big for her legs so she put them on the tops of her arms and went running back to the house with the butterfly tags flying in the wind.

The next day the Mungoes took the ferry home and Mr Mungoe and Mrs Mungoe and James all said that Great Uncle Fergus's Seventy-fifth Birthday Party was something they would never forget. Hetty said nothing, but she waved her blue spotty handkerchief, as if it were the Scottish flag itself, at G.U.F. and at Robin, who came with him, and whose socks had fallen down to his ankles because he had no garters.

Three weeks later a parcel arrived at the Mungoes' squeezed-in little terrace. It was addressed to Hetty. And inside was a kilt in blue, green and black tartan. *And* hairy socks. *And* garters with tartan butterfly tags. And this time they fitted.

There was a message too. It said, "To Hetty of the high heart" and underneath, in bold, black writing, "with love from Great Uncle Fergus, Chief!"